Good Dog

by Geraldine McCaughrean
Illustrated by Colin Smithson

Fife Council Education Department
King's Road Primary School
King's Crescent, Rosyth KY11 2RS

Fife
COUNCIL

One day the farmer brought home a dog
and tied him up in the yard.
"Good Dog," he said firmly.
"Now I want everyone to understand.
This isn't a pet. This is a working dog."

"No mamby-pamby baskets by the fire. No fussing and patting. No titbits off your plates."

"No silly games with sticks. A good work dog just fetches things for his master."

Good Dog barked and ran and fetched
the letters from the mat.
"That's the way!" said the farmer.

So Good Dog ran and fetched the newspaper.
"Good Dog!" said the farmer.

Out of the house ran Good Dog to fetch
a duck from the pond.
"That will do for today,"
said the farmer.

But Good Dog went on fetching things.
For instance, he fetched Gregorie Peck
the hen, and several dozen eggs.

Then he brought in Tally-Ho the horse and Blue Moo the cow.

He kindly brought the farmer's car right
to the front door, and the farm tractor, too.

Next morning, on the doorstep, there were nine pillar boxes and several lamp-posts.

Later Good Dog fetched a policeman who did not really want to come.

Neither did the passengers on the bus, nor the wild animals Good Dog fetched home from the zoo.

After that, Good Dog fetched the barn and the corn silo, too.

He found it quite difficult to get his jaws around Oxfordshire, but he brought all he could carry.

With a little digging, he even
fetched a river all the way
to the door.

He managed to find a giant in Fairyland
and a whole pirate crew, too.

"Stop!" said the farmer (not for the first time). "Take it all back, this instant!"

"But I'm a work dog. I only fetch things,"
said Good Dog and sat down on the mat.
"Now if I was a House Dog ..."

So the farmer told his family,
"Meet our new House Dog."
The children were very pleased.

20

After that, Good Dog protected the house wonderfully well. He drove off all the giants and wild animals. He saved the house from flooding. He frightened off the pirates and even the angry policeman.

The farmer told his friends,
"He's a wonderful House Dog, you know."

"I keep him by me always,
(just in case anyone should steal him)."

"And all he needs is a little exercise."